THIS BOOK
BELONGS TO:

_____

DATE RECEIVED: _____

Deep in the ocean, in the coral reef, among the shipwrecks and seaweed; the ocean creatures live and play. Here is what happened to them one warm and sunny day.

Stacey was stuck, very stuck, so stuck, in fact, that she couldn't even remember the last time she had moved. She didn't even like being stuck. She thought that maybe if she waited long enough, she might just become…unstuck. Her idea was not working.

For days on end, Stacey remained still. She would often see the other fish swim by laughing and having fun. Stacey would just eat any food that happened to float by her mouth. She only wished she could stretch her limbs, even for just a moment.

One day, a group of red fish were swimming by. They noticed Stacey and asked her if she would like to join them. "I would love to," said Stacey, "but you see, I am rather stuck to this rock."

"Stuck?" asked Radek the red fish. "How can that be? You have feet like all the other starfish. Do you not?"

"I suppose so," replied Stacey. "I just can't seem to get them to move. I have so many feet and none of them are working."

Radek thought for a moment about how he could help Stacey.

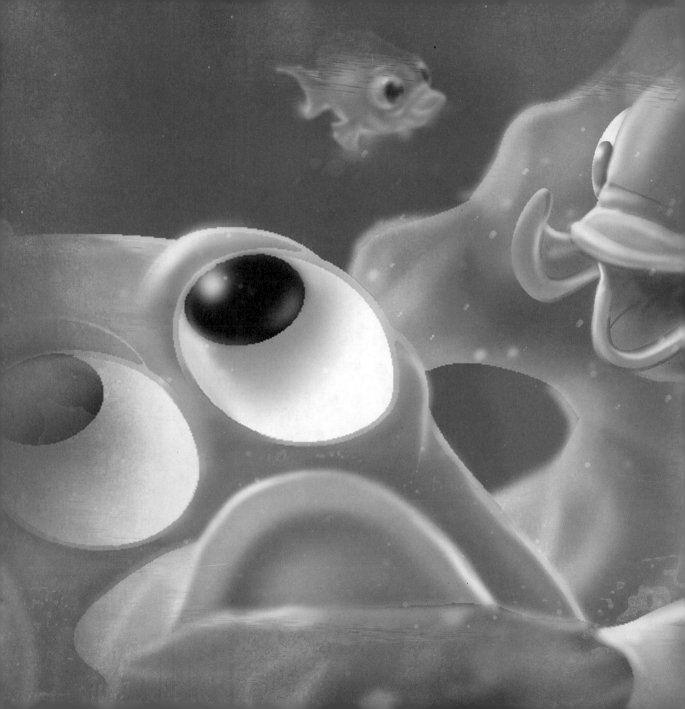

Suddenly, Radek had an idea. "Try moving just one foot first. Can you do that?" he asked. Stacey concentrated as hard as she could.

"There!" said Radek, "Did you see that? You moved one."

"I did, didn't I?" Stacey said excitedly.

"Yes, now try another!" said Radek.

Stacey tried as hard as she could to move another foot. Again, it moved. Soon she had the feet on one entire arm moving and completely unstuck.

"That's great!" said Radek. "Now, how about the rest?" Before long, Stacey had completely removed herself from the rock. She was about to give Radek a big hug when…

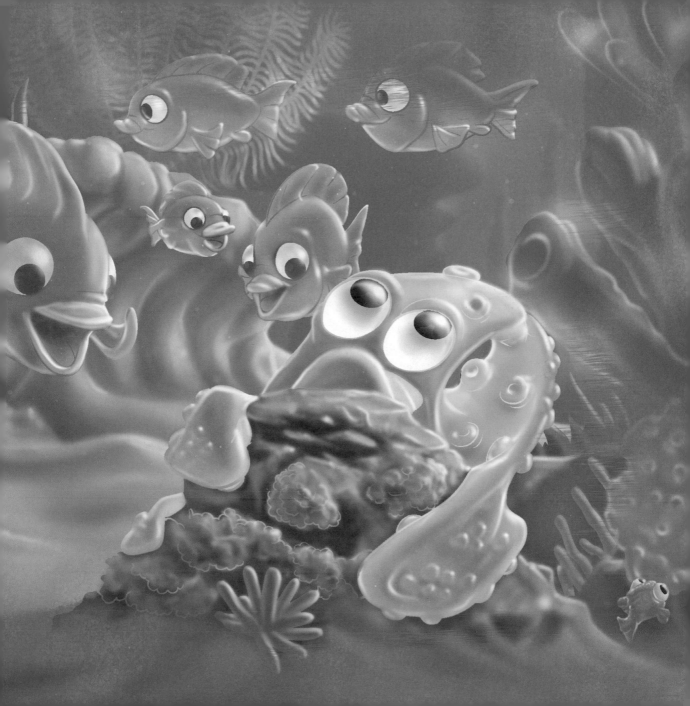

Suddenly a tide came through and carried Stacey off into the ocean. She floated and swooshed and floated some more. She floated to places she had never seen before. The entire time Stacey floated, she watched the new sights until she came to a stop.

Radek, and the rest of Stacey's ocean friends, immediately sent out search parties.

"She's around here somewhere," said Radek, "and we'll find her."

The group then heard Raymond Red Fish calling from near by. "Over here!" he said. "She's over here in this coral!"

Everyone raced over to see
if Stacey was alright. "Stacey!"
said Radek, "How are you? Are
you hurt?"

"No," replied Stacey, "in fact,
I feel wonderful!"

"What happened?" asked
Raymond. "Where did you go?"